Watson Caring
Science Institute

The Story of the Lotus Flower

Written by Jeremiah Bartsch MSN, RN-BC,
Certified Caritas Coach®

Illustrated by Walter Trush

Watson Caring Science Institute

ABOUT WATSON CARING SCIENCE INSTITUTE

We're here for nurses.

Watson Caring Science Institute (WCSI) is an international non-profit 501C(3) organization that advances the unitary philosophies, theories and practices of Caring Science, developed by Dr. Jean Watson, Ph.D., RN, AHN-BC, FAAN, LL (AAN). Watson's Caring Science is a trans-disciplinary approach that incorporates the art and science of nursing and includes concepts from the fields of philosophy, ethics, ecology and mindbody-spirit medicine.

Our work has proven to engage and retain nursing staff and dramatically improve patient's perception of care. Focusing on research, education, practice, legacy and leadership, WCSI deepens the development and understanding of Caring Science and Caritas Practices. As a result, we intentionally transform the patient/family experiences of caring and healing in schools, hospitals, the wider community and our planet.

The Institute has prepared nurses, healthcare workers, and health leaders worldwide to translate theory into authentic practice. Our Caritas Coaches® & Caritas Leaders® lead more than 3000,000 licensed nurses who care for over over a million patients per year in hospitals alone.

Gratitude and Dedication

Jeremiah would like to thank Dr. Jean Watson and Watson Caring Science Institute for wisdom and inspiration, without whom this book would not have been possible. Thank you to Walter for beautifully imagining this story and visually channeling my message. Gratitude for my Caritas Coach® sisters, Dana, Dianna, Julie, and Shelbie for sharing your thoughts, suggestions, and positivity. Above all, thank you to my extraordinary family Monique, Kaden, Kiah, Kallan and Kendyl – I love you!

Walter would like to thank: my always supportive and loving mother, Dianna Trush RN, OFS, Caritas Coach®

This book is dedicated to the mothers and fathers out there who are working hard to raise their children as best they can in such a crazy and often chaotic world. Keep shining the Light!

Do you know the story,

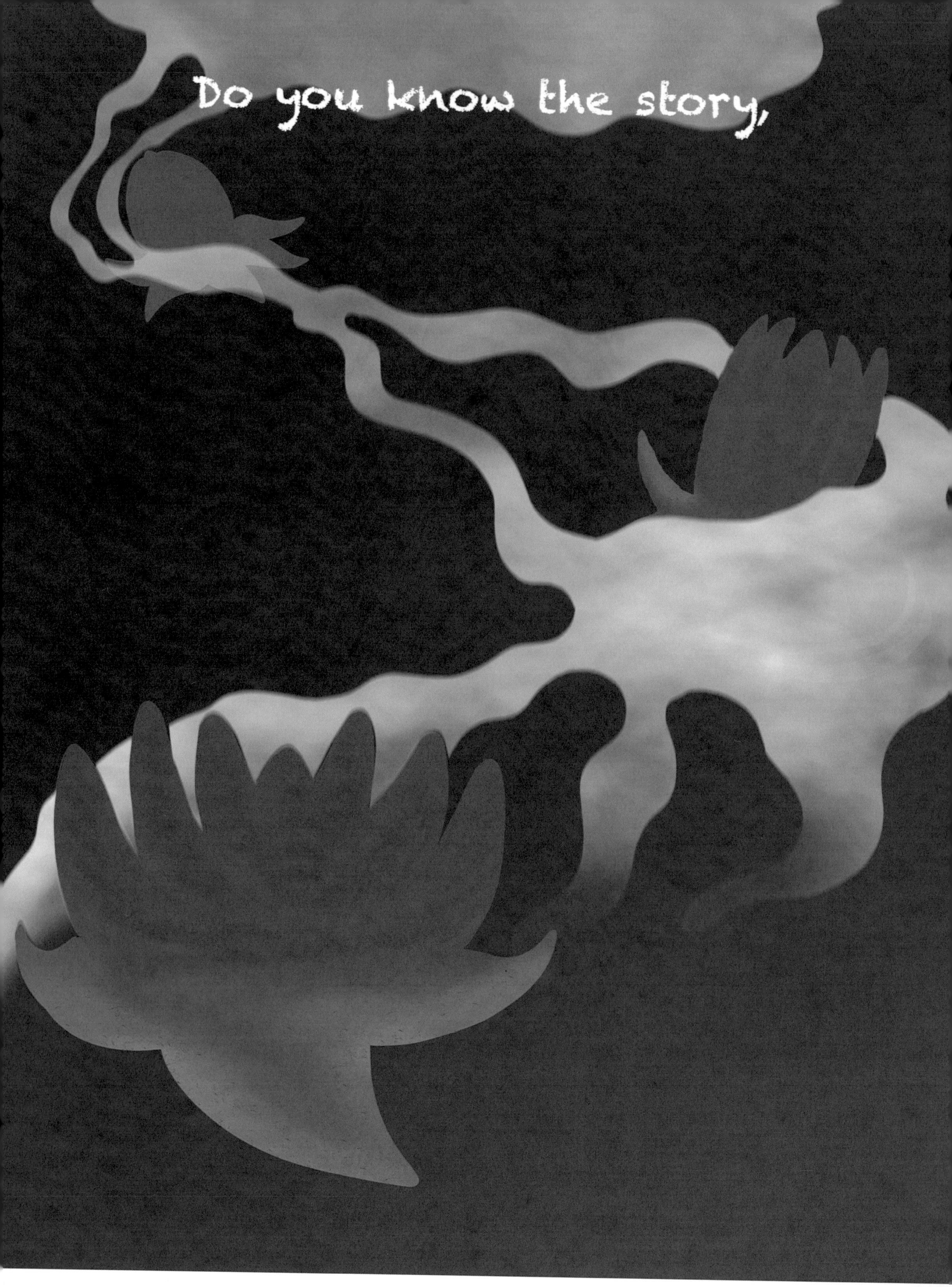

Of the beautiful lotus flower?

The lotus begins its life

Deep within the murky lake

Where from it comes?

And its magical power?

Scarcely touched by the sun

Growing; its beauty to awake

Rooted deep within the mud

An impossible path to tread

With strong determination

It journeys on ahead

Surface clear or covered in leaves

Water dark, pad of green

Until the flower surfaces

Its petals bright and clean

Wedding white, purple royal,

Pink and electric blue

There's yellow too and even red

Each one brilliant, glowing, new

Up from the muddy waters

Its beauty remains intact

This is no easy feat

It is magical, in fact

You see, the Lotus flower

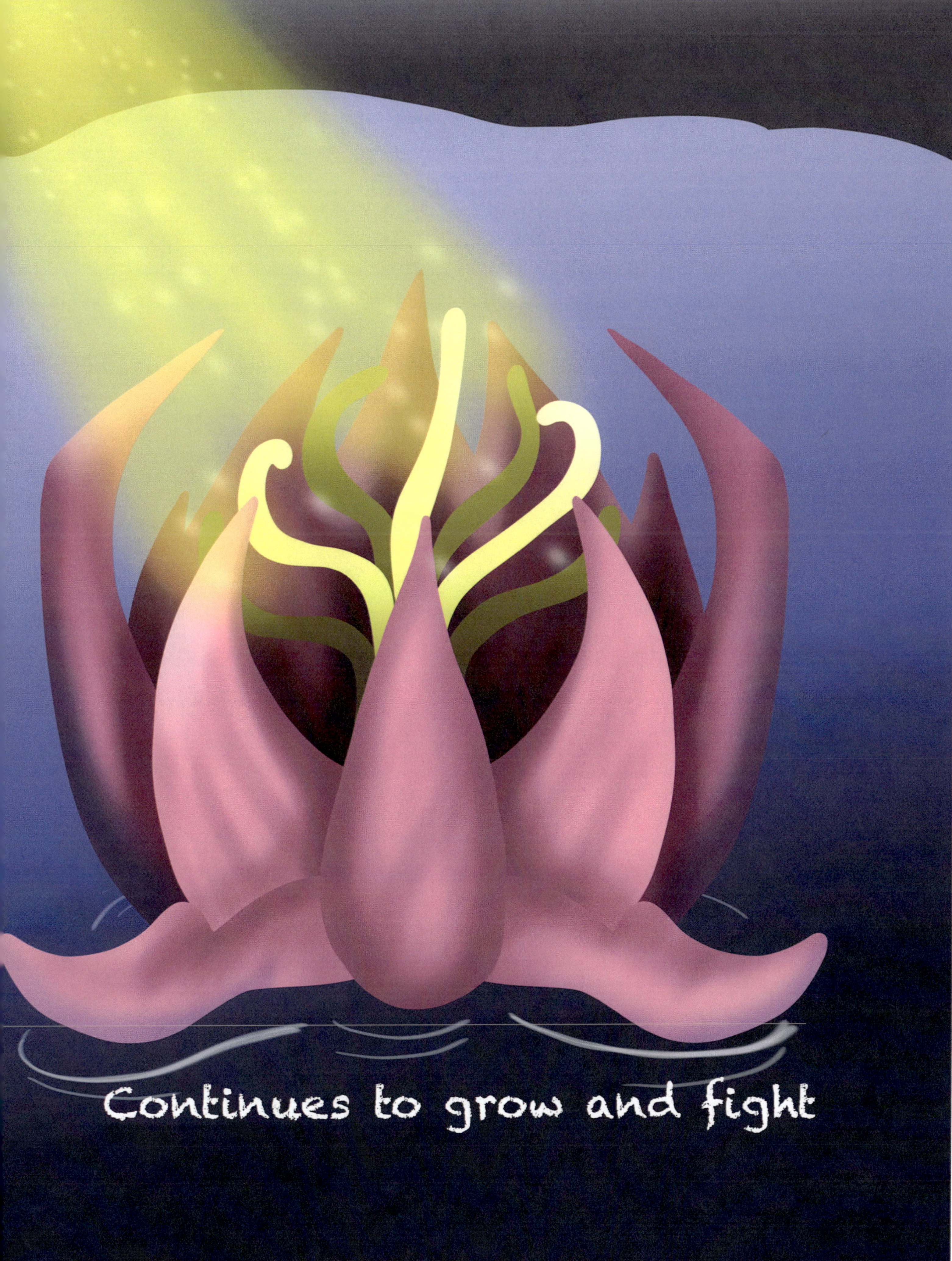
Continues to grow and fight

Unwavering perseverance

With or without an end in sight

Not overcome by a daunting task

Never giving in

It holds its head up high

A strength so deep within

When you feel overwhelmed

When you feel held back

Remember the lovely lotus

And keep yourself on track

Your beauty lies inside

Your wonderful strength runs deep

Keep yourself and mind centered

There are amazing rewards to reap

Remember, every journey

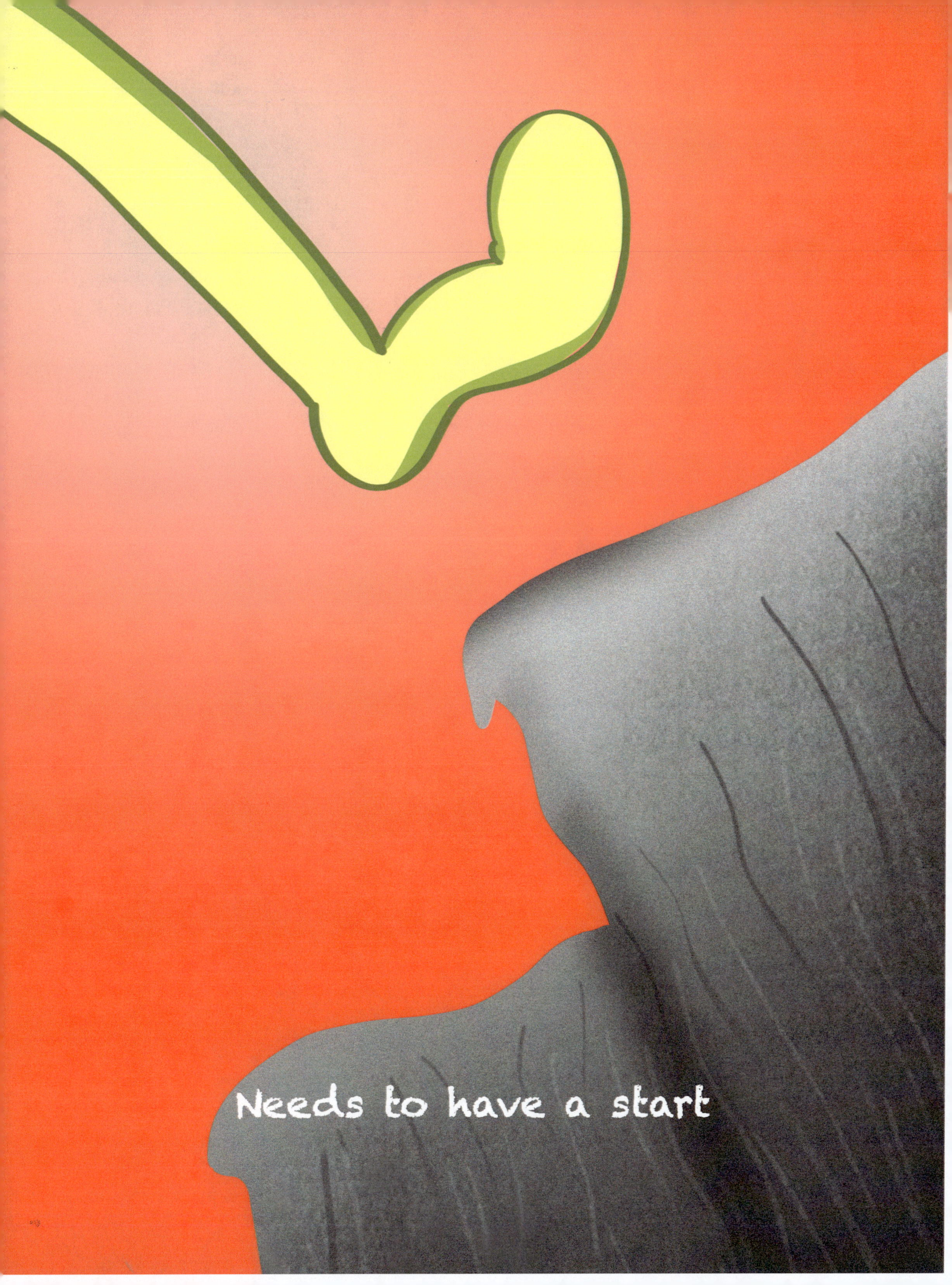

Needs to have a start

There's nothing that can stop you

Trust your caritas heart

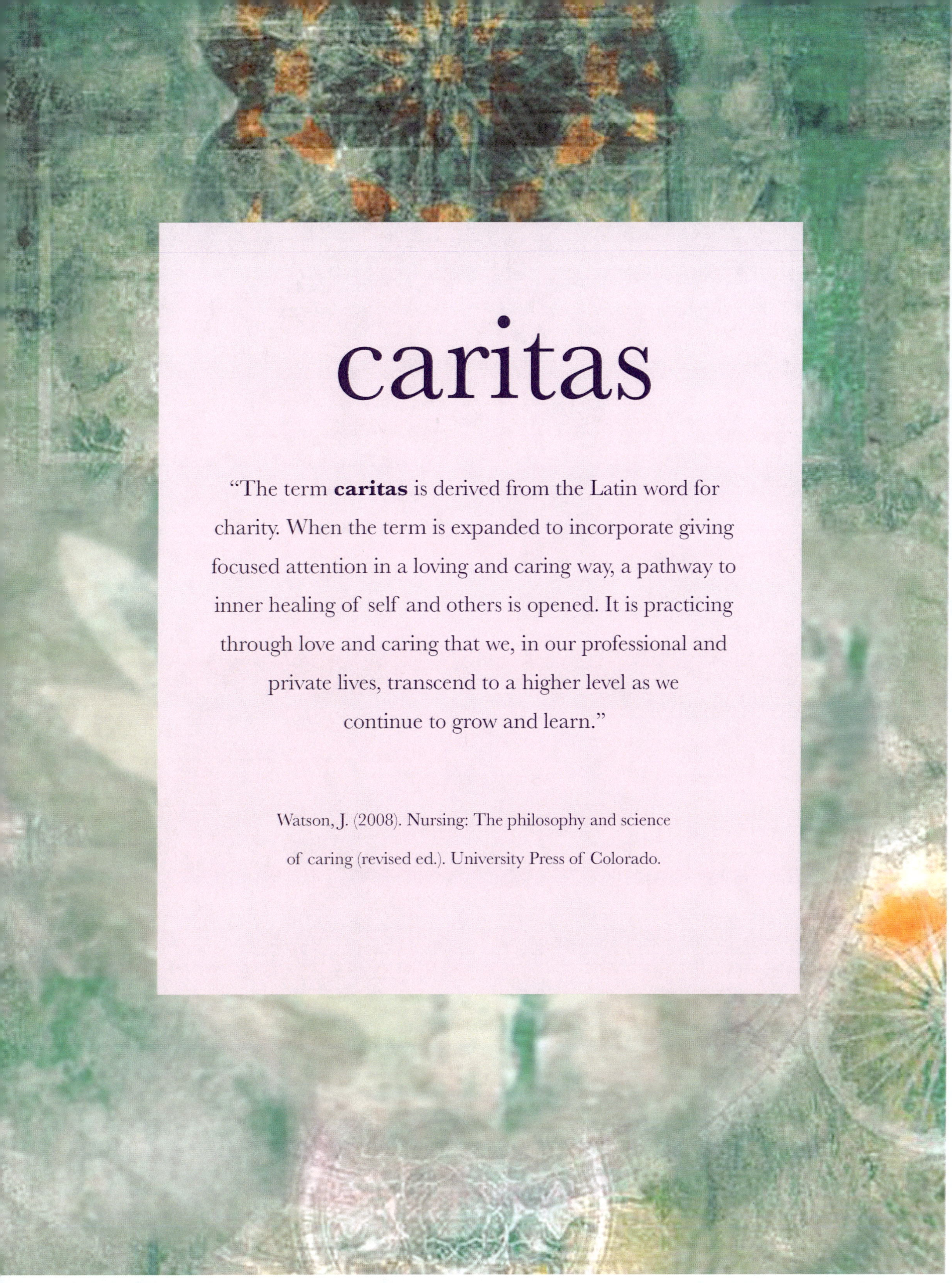

caritas

"The term **caritas** is derived from the Latin word for charity. When the term is expanded to incorporate giving focused attention in a loving and caring way, a pathway to inner healing of self and others is opened. It is practicing through love and caring that we, in our professional and private lives, transcend to a higher level as we continue to grow and learn."

Watson, J. (2008). Nursing: The philosophy and science of caring (revised ed.). University Press of Colorado.

ABOUT THE AUTHOR

Jeremiah Bartsch is a father, husband, and registered nurse living in rural Wisconsin. In 2001 he began his healthcare career in mental health, and since has had the opportunity to serve in several areas including skilled nursing, rehab, ICU, acute inpatient, and management. Jeremiah has a master's degree in nurse leadership and has earned many certifications. He is a Watson Caring Science Institute Caritas Coach® and serves as a Faculty Mentor. This is his first book.